DATE DUE			
MAR. 1 9 1993			
MAR. 1 9 1993			
NOV 22 '95			
SEP 23 99			
CZW 9/01			
SEP 2 8 2022			

LLAMA AND THE GREAT FLOOD

A Folktale from Peru

by Ellen Alexander

LLAMA AND THE GREAT FLOOD

A Folktale from Peru

by Ellen Alexander

Thomas Y. Crowell   New York

Special thanks to Dr. George L. Urioste, author of *Pariya Qaqa: La Tradi-ción Oral de Waru Chiri,* and to Dr. Sabine MacCormack, who helped clarify some historical references.

Library of Congress Cataloging-in-Publication Data
Alexander, Ellen.
   Llama and the great flood.

   Summary: In this Peruvian myth about the
Great Flood, a llama warns his master of the
coming destruction and leads him and his
family to refuge on a high peak in the Andes.
   1. Deluge—Juvenile literature.
2. Mythology, Peruvian—Juvenile literature.
[1. Mythology, Peruvian] I. Title.
BL325.D4A43 1989   299'.8   88-1194
ISBN 0-690-04727-4
ISBN 0-690-04729-0 (lib. bdg.)

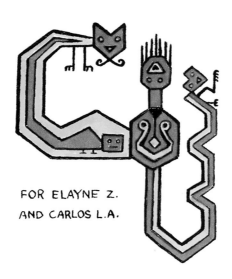

FOR ELAYNE Z.
AND CARLOS L.A.

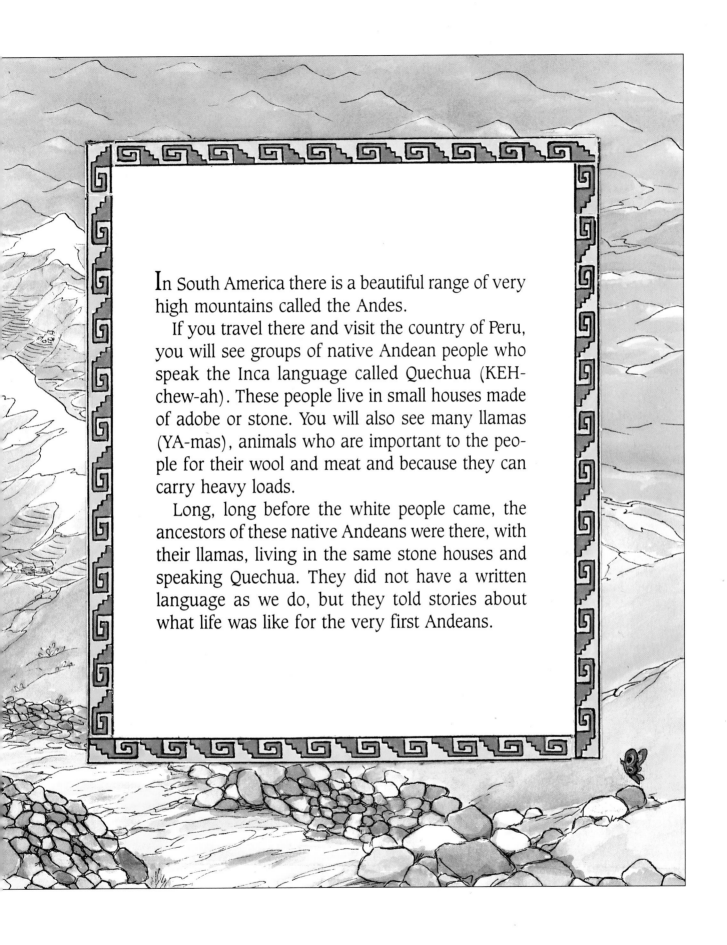

In South America there is a beautiful range of very high mountains called the Andes.

If you travel there and visit the country of Peru, you will see groups of native Andean people who speak the Inca language called Quechua (KEH-chew-ah). These people live in small houses made of adobe or stone. You will also see many llamas (YA-mas), animals who are important to the people for their wool and meat and because they can carry heavy loads.

Long, long before the white people came, the ancestors of these native Andeans were there, with their llamas, living in the same stone houses and speaking Quechua. They did not have a written language as we do, but they told stories about what life was like for the very first Andeans.

The Quechua people of Peru say that during ancient times,
before the coming of the god Viracocha, this world
reached a point at which it was about to end.

A certain llama who was living high up in the
Andes Mountains knew what was about to happen.

He had a dream in which he saw the sea overflow
and flood the whole world.

This dream upset the llama so that he could not eat.
He just walked around day after day, crying.

He acted this way even though his thoughtful owner
had given him a beautiful meadow to graze in.

The llama soon began growing thin, and his owner
worried about him and then started to become angry.

Finally, the man threw an ear of corn at the llama
and shouted, "Why don't you eat, you foolish animal?

15

"I allow you to graze in this beautiful meadow
and you just stand there and cry!"

The llama looked at him and with great sadness in his voice answered in the man's language, "It is YOU who are the fool!

"Don't you know what is happening? Within five days the sea will overflow!

"Yes, it's true! The world will be destroyed!"

19

The man was frightened, and he cried out to the llama,
"What will become of us? How can we save ourselves?"

The llama answered, "Let us go to the top of Willka Qutu. There we will be safe. But bring enough food for five days."

The man hurried home to tell his wife and gather food.
Then the family hurried off to the highest mountain.

When they reached the top of Willka Qutu,
they saw gathered there animals of every kind.

There were more llamas, alpacas and guanacos,
lions and foxes, tiny mice and great condors.

There were sheep, armadillos, colorful macaws,
and every other type of animal that lived.

Almost at once the sea began to overflow
and they all remained stranded there.

The sea covered all the other mountain peaks.
Only the top of Willka Qutu remained above water.

It is said that the water even reached the fox's tail
and turned it black. It is still that color today.

At the end of five long, cold days, the sea went down again and everything began to dry out.

When the sea had gone all the way down,
it could be seen that there were no more

people or animals left in the world.

Except for those people and animals who were watching all of this from the top of Willka Qutu.

Slowly, they began climbing down,
until they stood once more in the meadows and valleys.

The people began rebuilding their house of stone, and the corral for their llama. They planted corn and potatoes.

Soon many new people and animals were born into the world,
and all were children of those on Willka Qutu.

The Andean people still speak of the great flood,
and they believe that it was Willka Qutu

and the llama who saved them from destruction.

Llama and the Great Flood was inspired by a collection of myths from Huarochirí, a mountainous region northeast of Lima, Peru. These myths, which were originally told in the Quechua language, describe the earliest times of the people and tell of a great flood that destroyed almost every living thing on Earth.

The story of a great flood is found in myths and histories all over the world, including the story of Noah's Ark in the book of Genesis, and the myths of Greece and Rome. The Huarochirí version was changed somewhat by the Spanish historians of the sixteenth century, however, and as a result we do not know exactly when the flood was supposed to have happened in that region.

We do not know what type of clothing or other objects an Andean family would have had then, so I have used articles and designs from several pre-Inca cultures such as the Wari and the Moche. The

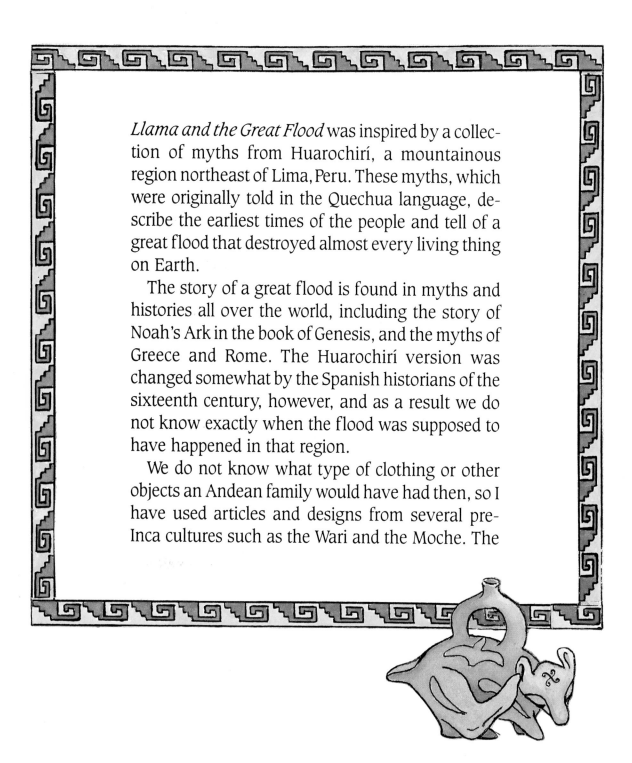

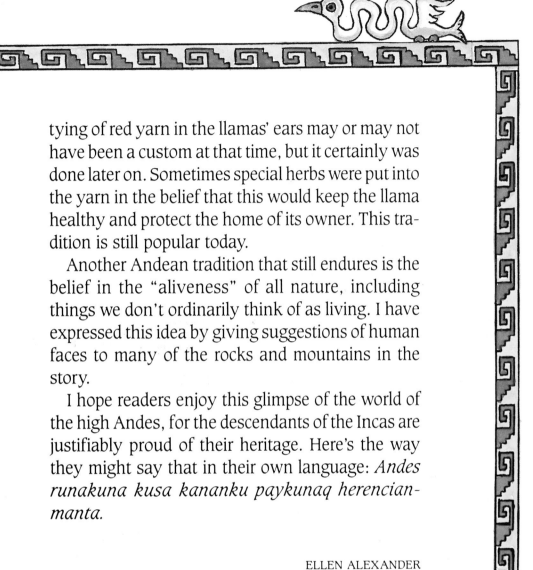

tying of red yarn in the llamas' ears may or may not have been a custom at that time, but it certainly was done later on. Sometimes special herbs were put into the yarn in the belief that this would keep the llama healthy and protect the home of its owner. This tradition is still popular today.

Another Andean tradition that still endures is the belief in the "aliveness" of all nature, including things we don't ordinarily think of as living. I have expressed this idea by giving suggestions of human faces to many of the rocks and mountains in the story.

I hope readers enjoy this glimpse of the world of the high Andes, for the descendants of the Incas are justifiably proud of their heritage. Here's the way they might say that in their own language: *Andes runakuna kusa kananku paykunaq herencianmanta.*

ELLEN ALEXANDER

39